Now look at her garden.

That's curious, too.

Isn't it?

Now look at Little Miss Curious.

She's rather curious looking, too.

And she also has a very curious
nature.

She wants to know the
how?
why?
and
what?
of everything.

One day, Little Miss Curious
set off for town.

"Why do doors squeak, but are not small
and furry with pink ears and long tails?"
she asked her door as she went out.

Understandably, the door didn't answer.

"Why do flowers live in beds but never sleep?" she asked the flowers in her garden.

They just smiled, knowingly.

Then she saw a worm.
"Why do worms in Nonsenseland wear
bow-ties?" she asked.

"That's for me to know and you to find
out about," said the worm, laughing.

Later, on the way to town,
Little Miss Curious met
Mr Nonsense.

Are you curious to find out
what she asked him?

Well go on then, turn over!

"I'm curious..." began Little Miss Curious, "...to know why it is that sandwiches are called sandwiches if they don't have any sand in them."

"It just so happens," said Mr Nonsense, "that this is a **sand** sandwich. I'm rather partial to sand!"

"Happy Christmas," he said.

Then Mr Nonsense ran away holding his sandwich carefully so that the sand didn't fall out.

Little Miss Curious eventually arrived
in town.

Did I hear you ask, "Why?"

Well, you are curious,
aren't you?

But are you as curious as
Little Miss Curious?

Little Miss Curious had gone to
town to visit the library.

"I wonder, would you be able to
help me?" she asked.

"Of course," said Mrs Page, the librarian.
"What are you looking for?"

"I'm looking for a book," began
Little Miss Curious,
"a book that will tell me
why the sky is blue..."

"...and why combs have teeth,
but can't bite,
...and why chairs have legs,
but can't play football,
...and why..."

And she went on,
and on,
and on,
until there was a very long queue
behind her, that was growing longer
by the minute.

"That's enough!" cried Mrs Page.

"NEXT PLEASE!"

"But why..." Little Miss Curious started to ask.

But without quite knowing how or why,
she suddenly found herself out in the street.

"How curious," Little Miss Curious
thought to herself.

As she walked along the street,
Little Miss Curious asked herself:
"Why is everybody giving me
such curious looks?
And why is Little Miss Careful waving
her umbrella at me?
Is it because it's going to rain?"

We don't think so, do we?

Little Miss Curious ran off.

Are you going to ask, "Why?"

Are you becoming as curious as
Little Miss Curious?

Can you guess
where she ran off to?

Neither can I.

Come back Little Miss Curious
and tell us where you're going!

You see, we're all ever so curious.

Yes, really we are!

3 Great Offers for MR. MEN Fans!

MR. MEN TOKEN

1 New Mr. Men or Little Miss Library Bus Presentation Cases

A brand new stronger, roomier school bus library box, with sturdy carrying handle and stay-closed fasteners.
The full colour, wipe-clean boxes make a great home for your full collection.
They're just £5.99 inc P&P and free bookmark!

☐ MR. MEN ☐ LITTLE MISS (please tick and order overleaf)

2 Door Hangers and Posters

In every Mr. Men and Little Miss book like this one, you will find a special token. Collect 6 tokens and we will send you a brilliant Mr. Men or Little Miss poster and a Mr. Men or Little Miss double sided full colour bedroom door hanger of your choice. Simply tick your choice in the list and tape a 50p coin for your two items to this page.

PLEASE STICK YOUR 50P COIN HERE

Door Hangers (please tick)
☐ Mr. Nosey & Mr. Muddle
☐ Mr. Slow & Mr. Busy
☐ Mr. Messy & Mr. Quiet
☐ Mr. Perfect & Mr. Forgetful
☐ Little Miss Fun & Little Miss Late
☐ Little Miss Helpful & Little Miss Tidy
☐ Little Miss Busy & Little Miss Brainy
☐ Little Miss Star & Little Miss Fun

Posters (please tick)
☐ MR. MEN
☐ LITTLE MISS

CUT ALONG DOTTED LINE AND RETURN THIS WHOLE PAGE

3 Sixteen Beautiful Fridge Magnets – any 2 for £2.00! inc.P&P

They're very special collector's items!
Simply tick your first and second* choices from the list below
of any 2 characters!

1st Choice
- ☐ Mr. Happy
- ☐ Mr. Lazy
- ☐ Mr. Topsy-Turvy
- ☐ Mr. Bounce
- ☐ Mr. Bump
- ☐ Mr. Small
- ☐ Mr. Snow
- ☐ Mr. Wrong
- ☐ Mr. Daydream
- ☐ Mr. Tickle
- ☐ Mr. Greedy
- ☐ Mr. Funny
- ☐ Little Miss Giggles
- ☐ Little Miss Splendid
- ☐ Little Miss Naughty
- ☐ Little Miss Sunshine

2nd Choice
- ☐ Mr. Happy
- ☐ Mr. Lazy
- ☐ Mr. Topsy-Turvy
- ☐ Mr. Bounce
- ☐ Mr. Bump
- ☐ Mr. Small
- ☐ Mr. Snow
- ☐ Mr. Wrong
- ☐ Mr. Daydream
- ☐ Mr. Tickle
- ☐ Mr. Greedy
- ☐ Mr. Funny
- ☐ Little Miss Giggles
- ☐ Little Miss Splendid
- ☐ Little Miss Naughty
- ☐ Little Miss Sunshine

*Only in case your first choice is out of stock.

--- **TO BE COMPLETED BY AN ADULT** ---

To apply for any of these great offers, ask an adult to complete the coupon below and send it with
the appropriate payment and tokens, if needed, to MR. MEN CLASSIC OFFER, PO BOX 715, HORSHAM RH12 5WG

☐ Please send _____ Mr. Men Library case(s) and/or _____ Little Miss Library case(s) at £5.99 each inc P&P

☐ Please send a poster and door hanger as selected overleaf. I enclose six tokens plus a 50p coin for P&P

☐ Please send me _____ pair(s) of Mr. Men/Little Miss fridge magnets, as selected above at £2.00 inc P&P

Fan's Name _____

Address _____

_____ **Postcode** _____

Date of Birth _____

Name of Parent/Guardian _____

Total amount enclosed £ _____

☐ **I enclose a cheque/postal order payable to Egmont Books Limited**

☐ **Please charge my MasterCard/Visa/Amex/Switch or Delta account** (delete as appropriate)

Card Number

Expiry date ___/___ **Signature** _____

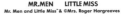

MR.MEN LITTLE MISS
Mr. Men and Little Miss™ & ©Mrs. Roger Hargreaves

CUT ALONG DOTTED LINE AND RETURN THIS WHOLE PAGE

Stockton Borough Public Libraries